GW00866454

ABOUT THE AUTHOR

Matt Black is a singer-songwriter, multi-instrumentalist, artist, writer and performer.

Born in 1986, in the small town of Barnsley, South Yorkshire.

Matt has been part of the music industry as a performer and writer from the age of sixteen. He is the front man of hard rock / metal group 'Fahran' based in the UK.

This book is dedicated to every human with a beautiful heart.

Share your kindness, love and friendship with those who need it most.

Be yourself, and be supportive to others.

X

Rikki The Rockstar

Written by Matt Black

Illustrations by Lucy Gilbert

Edited by Emily Irwe

Rikki Rad is a teenager in England. Rikki loves to sing and play guitar!

He had always dreamed of being a Rockstar. Rikki would play all across the land with his band: Crash Banger on drums and Al 'Alto' Note on bass.

One night, Rikki and his band were playing a show, and special visitor came to see them.

The special visitor was a man from a record company.

I love your songs!! I can make all your dreams come true...

I've waited for this all my life!

I am so excited!!!!!!

It's actually happening!!

He promised to put them on the radio and let them see the world.

Rikki became famous! His face was on every magazine, and his songs were on the radio everyday.

He bought a big house, fancy cars, and he could do anything he wanted!

Everyone wanted to know Rikki, but they weren't real friends. They just wanted to make money from him and take photos with him so they would look cool.

Rikki said that he wanted to join his friends and be a band again. So he called Harry on the phone and asked if he would make the band famous. Harry said 'No'.

No!!!!!

Rikki told Harry that he would only sing again if he could be with his band. He stood up for his friends, and then Harry agreed to make them all famous!

Harry gave them money to record new songs. They were all so happy and worked hard together to make new music, even better than before!

The band played all over the world, and even took their friends and family with them. Everyone was smiling and having a fantastic time!

Rikki was so happy to be with his friends again. He learned that it is so important to care for your friends, and to look out for each other!

Rikki and the band played the biggest show of their lives, and everyone was proud of the person he had become!

Rikki Rad had become a good person, a loyal friend, and finally he became

Rikki The Rockstar!!!!

The End

HOW TO BE A GOOD FRIEND

Share your toys

Be polite

Don't make fun of people

Take turns

Say "I'm Sorry"

Be a good listener

Laugh together

Help each other

Be kind

Say "Good luck"

Give hugs

Thank you for reading Rikki The Rockstar

www.mattblackofficial.com
www.twitter.com/mattblackuk
www.facebook.com/mattblackvocalist
www.instagram.com/mattblackofficial

Printed in Great Britain
by Amazon